Soulful Creations: A Culinary Symphony of Passionate Recipes

Bety & Bruno's Cook and Bake Book with Passion Vol.1

Bety & Bruno

To our beloved friends and family, Congratulations! You've been officially drafted into our culinary army. We couldn't have asked for more willing taste testers, enthusiastic cheerleaders, and patient dishwashers.

To our dear friends, thanks for pretending to enjoy our experimental tofu lasagna (we promise to stick to real cheese next time).

To our loving families, thanks for not disowning us after that unfortunate incident with the flaming dessert (we've learned to leave the pyrotechnics to the professionals).

And to our trusty pans, you've seen us through thick and thin (and sometimes burnt to a crisp). Here's to many more sizzling adventures together!

Let's eat until our apron strings burst and our bellies sing with joy!

With love, laughter, and a sprinkle of flour,
Bety and Bruno

Acknowledgements

To our loyal taste testers, who bravely sampled our culinary experiments and lived to tell the tale (mostly).

To our pots and pans, for enduring countless hours of stirring, sautéing, and simmering without complaint (we promise to clean you more often).

To our spice cabinet, for adding a dash of excitement to every dish and occasionally surprising us with unexpected flavor combinations.

To our oven, for transforming our raw ingredients into golden-brown perfection, even when we accidentally set it to 'broil' instead of 'bake'.

To our cookbook collection, for providing endless inspiration and reminding us that even the greatest chefs started with burnt toast.

And most importantly, to each other, for embarking on this delicious adventure together, even when we disagreed on whether to add more garlic (spoiler alert: the answer is always yes).

Here's to many more culinary escapades, mishaps, and triumphs. Let's eat, laugh, and cook up some memories!

About the Authors

Meet Bruno, the culinary maestro with a family tree that's basically a linguistic buffet. Picture this: every family member born in different Portuguese-speaking countries in Asia and Africa. His food heritage is so untraditional Portuguese that it practically speaks Esperanto. Bruno's kitchen is an international passport stamped with flavor, from reinventing Italian pizzas to giving American recipes a makeover. Asian cuisine, however, is his true Everest = a challenge he embraces with chopsticks in hand.

But wait, there's more! Baking, for Bruno, is like a delicious time machine that whisks him back to his childhood. Family cakes and sweet dishes are not just recipes; they're treasured memories sprinkled with sugar. He's the guy who can turn a kitchen into a global dance floor, where flavors waltz, spices tango, and laughter does the cha-cha.

Now, let's talk about Bety. Hailing from the charming land of Portugal but raised amidst the Currywurst and Döner Kebap of Berlin, Bety is the embodiment of a cultural crossover. Her roots run deep, and so does her passion for whipping up traditional Portuguese dishes learned from the culinary elders in her family.

During the Pandemic plot twist, Bety did what any self-respecting food adventurer would do – she decided to conquer the German art of sourdough bread. Yes, you heard it right, folks, German-style sourdough! She called up her childhood friend in Berlin, probably interrupting their bratwurst brunch, to unlock the secrets of this mysterious bread-making universe. And just like that, Bety stumbled upon a whole new world of doughy delights, a world she fell in love with faster than you can say "Guten Appetit."

So here they are, Bruno and Bety, the dynamic culinary duo. One with a passport full of flavors, the other with a taste for tradition and a newfound love for German sourdough. Together, they're cooking up a storm, blending cultures, and turning the kitchen into a gastronomic carnival where every dish is a ticket to a world of taste bud ecstasy. Fasten your seatbelts, folks – it's going to be a delicious ride!

How the Story Begins...

Once upon a time in a kitchen far, far away, Bruno and I found ourselves on a culinary adventure unlike any other. Our parents, bless their hearts, expressed love through the magical medium of baking and cooking. While Bruno effortlessly fell head over heels for the sizzle and aroma of the kitchen, for me, it was merely a strategic means to impress or feed my perpetually hungry kids. My baking endeavors were legendary in their lack of success, and the idea of delving into the "whys" of my kitchen misadventures never crossed my mind.

Enter Bruno, the culinary wizard of our tale. His culinary skills, honed through countless readings and recipe redos, transformed ordinary ingredients into gastronomic masterpieces. My children, upon encountering his culinary wonders, declared his creations to be fit for a "Chef" and wondered aloud why he hadn't opened a restaurant.

Then came the fateful day when our lives collided, and Bruno moved in. In an attempt to shower us with affection, he baked up a storm every weekend. However, my kids and I, accustomed to considering food a mere survival necessity, failed to appreciate the sentiment behind his culinary gestures. Food was merely fuel, not an expression of love.

Cue the global pandemic, the ultimate plot twist. As we spent more time together, discussing feelings, life, and desires, we stumbled upon the heart of the matter - our differing tastes and expectations in the realm of food. A candid conversation unfolded, revealing my aversion to overly sweet cakes and my strict no-eating-after-8-pm policy. This revelation sparked a culinary revolution.

What followed was a whirlwind of recipe sharing and taste testing. Imagine original Carbonara with homemade pasta, Guanciale and Pecorino cheese = a culinary conundrum that needed addressing. We embarked on a journey of culinary compromise, reinventing our approach to recipes and food. Through trial and error, we uncovered the joy of healthier choices, the wonders of various flours, and the magic of sourdough.

In our kitchen, laughter became the secret ingredient, and love seasoned every dish, cake, and loaf of bread we shared with family and friends. Their encouragement became the catalyst for sharing our newfound techniques and recipes with the world. And so, our once mundane kitchen transformed into the stage for a delightful culinary performance = a story of reinvention, shared recipes, and the magic that happens when love and passion meet a hot stove. Welcome to our whimsical world of creative baking and cooking - a journey sparked by a pandemic, flavored with love, and spiced with laughter.

Bety & Bruno

Introduction:

"Dive into the tantalizing world of 'Soulful Creations,' where every page whispers the secrets of heartfelt cooking and the artistry of baking. This enchanting cookbook is a vibrant tapestry of passion, flavor, and culinary creativity, carefully woven together by a masterful chef with an undying love for the art of cooking.

Within these pages, you'll discover a treasure trove of passionate recipes that go beyond the ordinary, elevating the act of cooking into a soul-stirring experience. From decadent chocolate cakes that melt in your mouth to artisanal sourdough bread with a crispy crust that sings with each bite, each recipe is a testament to the author's unwavering devotion to the craft.

Embark on a journey through the aromatic world of freshly baked bread, where the symphony of crackling crusts and soft, pillowy interiors comes to life. Indulge your senses with velvety cheesecakes adorned with vibrant fruits and delicate drizzles of syrup, and experience the warmth of home-cooked stews that have been passed down through generations.

But 'Soulful Creations' is more than just a cookbook; it's a culinary love letter. Interspersed among the recipes are heartfelt stories, personal anecdotes, and culinary wisdom that make each page a delightful adventure. The author's passion for the art of cooking shines through, turning this book into a source of inspiration for aspiring chefs and home cooks alike.

Whether you're a novice baker seeking the perfect cake recipe or an experienced cook looking for new flavors to explore, 'Soulful Creations' invites you to step into the kitchen with enthusiasm and creativity. Let these passionate recipes be your guiding stars as you embark on your own culinary odyssey, transforming ordinary ingredients into extraordinary dishes that dance on your taste buds and linger in your memory."

What Bruno says about Cups vs. Grams: A Hilarious Showdown!

In one corner, we have the rebellious Americans with their trusty cups, measuring everything from flour to sugar. They eyeball it, toss it in, and hope for the best. It's like a culinary game of chance = will it be a fluffy cake or a pancake disaster? Who knows!

And in the other corner, we have the meticulous Europeans with their precise grams and milliliters. They weigh everything down to the last speck of salt, as if their kitchen was a chemistry lab. Every recipe is a scientific experiment, and they won't settle for anything less than perfection.

Meanwhile, the British are sipping tea, trying to figure out if a "pinch" of salt is more or less than a "dash." They're caught in a culinary twilight zone, balancing on the fine line between tradition and confusion.

Oh, and let's not forget the Australians, who are down under not only geographically but also in the kitchen measurement chaos. They might use cups, grams, or even "handfuls," leaving the rest of the world scratching their heads and wondering, "How much is a handful, mate?"

In this epic battle of cups vs. grams, the kitchen is the arena, and hilarity ensues as bakers and cooks try to decipher recipes. Will the cupcakes rise, or will the soufflé flop? One thing's for sure – it's going to be a wild, flour-covered ride! May the best measurement win!

Bruno's Belgian Belly Laughs Waffles

Ingredients:

- 1 cup of flour (because measuring with laughter is imprecise)
- 1/4 cup of cornstarch (for that extra corny flavor)
- 1/2 teaspoon of baking powder (to lift your spirits)
- 1/4 teaspoon of baking soda (because we're rising to the occasion)
- 1/2 teaspoon of salt (just a pinch of humor)
- 1 cup of buttermilk (it's not just milk, it's buttermilk, darling)
- 1/3 cup of melted butter, unsalted (because waffles without butter are like jokes without punchlines)
- 1 egg, room temperature and separated (let the egg come out of its shell and shine)
- 1/4 cup – 1/2 cup of sugar (depends on how sweet your tooth is feeling)

- 1 1/2 teaspoons of vanilla bean paste (because vanilla extract is so last season)

Note:
  = 1 cup of flour: 120 grams
  = 1/4 cup of cornstarch: 30 grams
  = 1/2 teaspoon of baking powder: 2 grams
  = 1/4 teaspoon of baking soda: 1.5 grams
  = 1/2 teaspoon of salt: 4 grams
  = 1 cup of buttermilk: 240 grams
  = 1/3 cup of melted butter, unsalted: 75 grams
  = 1 egg: around 50 grams (the weight can vary slightly)
  = 1/4 cup = 1/2 cup of sugar: 50 grams – 100 grams (depending on sweetness preference)
  = 1 1/2 teaspoons of vanilla bean paste: 7.5 grams

Instructions:
1. In a bowl, beat the egg white until it's as stiff as your favorite dad joke. Set aside, but don't put it in a corner.

2. In a medium bowl, combine the flour, cornstarch, baking powder, baking soda, and salt. Mix well, like a DJ spinning waffle beats.
3. Add the buttermilk, melted butter, egg yolk, sugar, and vanilla. Mix just until combined. Don't overmix; we're making waffles, not drama.
4. Gently fold in the egg whites. We're not making a soufflé; we just want those waffles to have a little fluff.
5. Let the batter sit for 30 minutes. Use this time to practice your waffle dance moves.
6. Heat a waffle iron. It's about to get hot in the waffle kitchen!
7. Follow the directions on your waffle iron to cook the waffles. Pretend you're a waffle chef and twirl around while doing it.
8. Serve immediately or keep warm in a 200-degree oven. Don't stack them; they're delicate, not pancakes.

Notes:
- To freeze, allow the waffles to cool completely and wrap them individually in plastic wrap. It's like giving your waffles a cozy winter coat.

- To reheat, just toss those frozen delights into the toaster. It's the waffle spa treatment.
- If you're into sweet comedy, go for the full 1/2 cup of sugar. If not, keep it a bit tamer.
- Depending on the size of your waffle iron, you might get 5-6 waffles. If your iron is smaller, well, just tell people you're serving "mini stand-up" waffles. They'll love it.

Bety's Berrylicious Comedy Cake

Timing:

Time Prep: 25 minutes (or until you run out of hilarious anecdotes)

Time Bake: 40-45 minutes (enough time to practice your stand-up routine)

Ingredients:

- 300g Blueberries (because life is better in blue)
- 150g Raspberries (for that extra berry excitement)
- 280g all-purpose flour (550 Weizen or T55, because numbers make it sound official)
- 8g baking powder (for a cake that rises to the occasion like a good joke)
- 180g unsalted butter - room temperature (let it be as soft as a comedian's heart)
- 90g white sugar (because sweetness is not optional)
- 4 eggs (S) - 220-230g (weigh them, but don't ask them about their feelings)
- 30g Sour Cream + 20ml half-skimmed milk (or 50ml fat milk, because comedy needs some dairy)

- Juice of half a lemon (25 ml, to add a tangy twist to your taste buds)
- 2 teaspoons of vanilla extract (because vanilla is not boring in this comedy show)
- Powdered sugar for dusting (for the grand finale)

Note:
- 300g Blueberries: Approximately 2 cups
- 150g Raspberries: Approximately 1 cup
- 280g all-purpose flour: Approximately 2 1/4 cups
- 8g baking powder: Approximately 2 teaspoons
- 180g unsalted butter: Approximately 3/4 cup
- 90g white sugar: Approximately 1/2 cup
- 4 eggs (220-230g): Approximately 1 cup
- 30g Sour Cream + 20ml half-skimmed milk: Approximately 1/4 cup Sour Cream + 1/8 cup (2 tablespoons) half-skimmed milk
- Juice of half a lemon (25ml): Approximately 2 tablespoons
- 2 teaspoons of vanilla extract: 2 teaspoons

Prep:

1. Preheat the oven to 180°C (350°F) and grease a 26cm diameter cake pan (10 inches, because size matters in baking, and comedy).
2. In a bowl, mix the butter and sugar until it's a creamy comedy duo.
3. Add the eggs one by one and mix them well after each addition, like a perfect comedic timing.
4. Stir in vanilla extract and the lemon juice = the dynamic flavor duo.
5. Mix the flour with the baking powder and separately mix the milk with the sour cream = because we like our ingredients to mingle before the show.
6. Add the dry and liquid ingredients alternately into the butter-egg-sugar mix. It's a batter comedy mix.
7. Mix all until it gets creamy smooth, just like a comedian's delivery.
8. In separate bowls, wash the blueberries & raspberries, but don't dry them. Moisture is the secret ingredient.
9. Pour half of the cake batter into the cake pan and spread half of the blueberries evenly without overlapping = it's all about sharing the spotlight.

10. Pour the remaining batter over the blueberries and distribute it evenly - everyone gets their moment.
11. Top around the outside circle with blueberries and the inner circle with raspberries - because every cake deserves a fruity audience.
12. Bake the cake in the preheated oven between 40-45 minutes until it turns golden brown. Check it after 40 minutes with a toothpick inserted in the middle – if it comes out clean, your cake is the headliner.
13. Dust the cake with powdered sugar and remove the pan after 10 minutes of cooling down – because a great cake deserves a standing ovation.

Bety's Nutty Banana Stand-Up Loaf

Timing:

Time Prep: 30 minutes (or until you've told at least three banana jokes)

Baking Time: 60 minutes (the  time it takes for your loaf to become the star of the oven show)

Ingredients:

- 350 grams ripe Madeira bananas (after peeling, because unpeeled bananas are the worst comedians)
- 30 grams sourdough starter (because even bread needs a kickstart)
- 2 eggs (about 115 grams, or two stand-up comedians — weigh them, but don't ask about their feelings)
- 100 grams liquid brown butter (not salted, because we're keeping it smooth) - 110 grams

in the pan to heat (let it sizzle, but not too dramatic)

- 80 grams brown cane sugar (for that sweet punchline)
- 180 grams flour (wheat T55/550, rice, or spelt 630 - because variety is the spice of loaf)
- 200 grams sour cream or creme fraiche (because banana bread likes to be a bit fancy)
- 1 teaspoon salt (just a pinch, we're not hosting a salty roast)
- 0.5 grams grated nutmeg (the tiniest bit, like a subtle background comedian)
- 6 grams baking powder (for that extra lift in your loaf's performance)
- 1 gram cinnamon (because banana and cinnamon are the comedy duo we all need)
- 100 grams nuts of your choice (because every good loaf needs a nutty entourage)

Note:
- 350 grams ripe Madeira bananas: Approximately 1.5 cups mashed bananas
- 30 grams sourdough starter: Approximately 2 tablespoons

- 2 eggs (about 115 grams): Approximately 1 cup (about 4 large eggs)
- 100 grams liquid brown butter: Approximately 7 tablespoons
- 110 grams in the pan to heat (let it sizzle, but not too dramatic)
- 80 grams brown cane sugar: Approximately 1/2 cup
- 180 grams flour (wheat T55/550, rice, or spelt 630): Approximately 1.5 cups
- 200 grams sour cream or creme fraiche: Approximately 1 cup
- 1 teaspoon salt: Approximately 1 teaspoon
- 0.5 grams grated nutmeg: Approximately 1/8 teaspoon
- 6 grams baking powder: Approximately 1.5 teaspoons
- 1 gram cinnamon: Approximately 1/2 teaspoon
- 100 grams nuts of your choice: Approximately 1 cup chopped nuts

Instructions:

1. Preheat the oven to 170 degrees Celsius (fan). Grease a loaf pan with butter and dust it with a thin layer of flour. Make that pan feel special!

2. Melt around 110 grams of unsalted butter in a pan until it gets brown. Let it cool down in the bowl for 10 minutes. We're looking for that golden-brown butter, not a burnt-toast comedy act.

3. Roast the nuts in another pan without fat until light brown. Give them a little toasting applause.

4. In the bowl, mix the eggs & the brown sugar with melted butter, beating until creamy with a whisk. This is the opening act, and we're going for a smooth performance.

5. Mash the bananas roughly with a fork, leaving some coarse pieces. Add the mashed bananas and cinnamon to the mixture in the bowl. Let the banana comedy unfold.

6. After, add the sour cream, the salt, the sourdough, and the nutmeg. It's a diverse cast of characters — let them mingle.

7. Sift the flour into another bowl and mix it with salt and baking powder. Gradually combine the dry mixture with the wet ingredients until

a homogeneous batter forms. It's all about the perfect comedy ensemble.

8. Add the roasted nuts to the batter. They're the surprise guests bringing the nutty flavor to the banana comedy show.

9. Bake the banana bread for about one hour at 170°C. Check around the 35-minute mark to see if the top of the banana bread is getting too dark. If it is, cover it with a sheet of aluminum foil and continue baking. If you prefer a very moist result, bake for a total of 50 minutes. For a slightly drier texture, bake for 60 minutes. It's your banana bread, so you're the director of this culinary comedy film!

Bruno & Bety's Stand-Up Lemon Chia Cupcake Extravaganza

Prep Time: 20 minutes (or until you've rehearsed your best lemon jokes)
Cook Time: 25 minutes (or until the cupcakes are cooked to perfection, unlike some punchlines)

Lemon Cupcake with Poppy Seeds

Ingredients:

- Four eggs (250g, because we like our eggs as a comedy quartet)
- 120g cups of white sugar (for that sweet symphony)
- 220g of softened butter (because a soft buttery entrance is the key to any good show)
- 240g of warm fat milk (because cold milk just doesn't get the applause)
- 240g cups of all-purpose flour (for an all-around good time)

- Zest of three lemons (because life needs more zest)
- 15g of poppy seeds (for that pop of surprise)
- 4g of baking powder (to lift the spirits of the cupcakes)

Note:
- Four eggs (250g): Approximately 1 cup
- 120g cups of white sugar: Approximately 2/3 cup
- 220g of softened butter: Approximately 1 cup (2 sticks)
- 240g of warm fat milk: Approximately 1 cup
- 240g cups of all-purpose flour: Approximately 1 3/4 cups
- Zest of three lemons: Approximately 3 tablespoons
- 15g of poppy seeds: Approximately 2 tablespoons
- 4g of baking powder: Approximately 1 teaspoon

Instructions:

1. Beat the egg yolks with sugar and butter - give them a pep talk, they're the opening act!

2. Add, without beating, warm milk, all-purpose flour, lemon zest, poppy seeds, and baking powder. No beating here; we're creating a smooth collaboration.

3. Beat the mixture for two minutes - it's the cupcake beatbox session.

4. Separately, beat the egg whites until stiff peaks form and fold into the mixture - this is the cupcake acrobatics part.

5. Pour the batter into greased cupcake forms and bake in a preheated oven at 180°C (350°F) for 25 minutes, or until a toothpick inserted into the center comes out clean. It's the cupcake's time to shine!

6. In a separate bowl, mix lemon juice with powdered sugar until well combined - the lemon glaze is the cupcake's red carpet moment.

7. Remove the cupcakes from the oven and unmold - it's the cupcake grand entrance.

Now, sit back, relax, and enjoy the laughter and lemony goodness of Bruno & Bety's Stand-Up Lemon Chia Cupcake Extravaganza!

Bety & Bruno's Love-Infused Laughter Granola

Prep Time: 15 minutes (or until you've shared a good joke with your oats)
Cook Time: 20-25 minutes (or until your granola is golden and full of joy)

Ingredients:

- 300g Oat (because oats are the comedians of the breakfast world)
- Pinch of salt (just a tiny pinch, we're not hosting a salty roast)
- 2 tablespoons of whey protein (any taste you like, because even protein needs to flex its flavor muscles)

- 60g corn syrup (if you want it crispy. If you prefer healthier, opt for honey - it's the sweet debate)
- 65g honey (because honey is the golden nectar of breakfast)
- 1 teaspoon vanilla extract (for that sweet symphony)
- 100g coconut oil (because coconut oil is the smooth operator)
- 130g nuts (we prefer a mix of almonds, pecans, hazelnuts, and peanuts = it's the nutty cast)

Note:
- 300g Oats: Approximately 3 cups
- Pinch of salt: Just a tiny pinch, no specific measurement
- 2 tablespoons of whey protein: Approximately 0.35 cups
- 60g corn syrup: Approximately 3 tablespoons
- 65g honey: Approximately 3 tablespoons
- 1 teaspoon vanilla extract: 1 teaspoon
- 100g coconut oil: Approximately 0.42 cups
- 130g nuts (mix of almonds, pecans, hazelnuts, and peanuts): Approximately 1.25 cups

Topping:

- 125g dark chocolate (we like 70%, because dark chocolate is the mysterious character)
- 75g goji (because goji berries are the superhero sidekick)

Note:

Instructions:

1. Preheat the oven to 160 degrees Celsius with convection. It's the warm-up for the granola show!

2. Mix in a bowl the oats, salt, whey protein, syrup/honey, vanilla, and coconut oil. Let the ingredients mingle like good friends at a comedy club.

3. Cut the nuts into smaller pieces and mix them into the bowl. It's the nutty ensemble joining the comedy lineup.

4. Spread the mixture evenly in a tray. It's time for the granola to take the stage.

5. Put it in the oven for 10 minutes, then mix it and spread again with a spoon. It's like a mid-show intermission, but for granola.

6. Let it go for 10 more minutes, mix it again with the spoon. The granola is rehearsing its crunchy routine.

7. Let it go for 5 more minutes and take it out to let it cool down. The granola deserves a standing ovation.

8. In the meanwhile, cut the chocolate bar into little pieces. When the granola mix is cold, mix the goji berries and chocolate. It's the grand finale.

9. Serve it with natural yogurt or açai. It's the encore, because this granola deserves an encore.

Enjoy Bety & Bruno's Love-Infused Laughter Granola – a breakfast that's so good, it'll have you laughing all day!

Bruno's Truffle Mushrooms Pasta: A Symphony of Italian Flavors

Time Prep: 30 minutes

Ingredients:

- 300 grams Portobello mushrooms
- 250 grams Tagliatelle dry pasta
- 400 ml Creme Fraiche
- 1 Shallot
- 2 cloves of garlic
- 1 small summer truffle
- 40 ml truffle-infused olive oil
- Salt and freshly ground black pepper
- Parmigiano Reggiano for finishing

Note:

- 300 grams Portobello mushrooms ≈ 2.5 cups (sliced)

- 250 grams Tagliatelle dry pasta ≈ 2.5 cups
- 400 ml Creme Fraiche ≈ 1.7 cups
- 1 Shallot ≈ 0.5 cups (finely chopped)
- 2 cloves of garlic ≈ 2 teaspoons (minced)
- 1 small summer truffle (size may vary, truffles are usually used in grams)
- 40 ml truffle-infused olive oil ≈ 2.7 tablespoons

Please note that these are approximate conversions, and the actual volume can vary based on factors like the specific ingredients, how they are packed, and your measuring techniques. Additionally, truffles are usually measured in grams because they are not easily converted into a volume measurement.

Preparation:
1. Begin by bringing a large pan of water to a lively boil, generously seasoned with salt. Introduce the pasta and let it dance until it achieves the perfect "al dente" performance.
2. Finely chop the shallot and garlic, setting the stage for the aromatic ensemble.
3. In a grand frying pan, set the heat to a captivating medium, and add the olive oil. Once

the stage is hot, introduce the shallot and garlic, orchestrating a symphony until they perform a delightful golden brown.

4. Cue the entrance of the chopped Portobello mushrooms, seasoned with the perfect harmony of salt and freshly ground black pepper. Let them sauté, stirring frequently, until they take on a beautiful brown hue.

5. Slice the truffle into fine notes, adding half to the mushroom melody and saving the other half for the grand finale.

6. Introduce the Creme Fraiche, allowing the composition to blend and thicken, a crescendo of flavors developing over a delightful 10-minute performance.

7. Drain the pasta, inviting it to join the mushroom orchestra. Turn off the heat, and let the pasta absorb the flavorful composition.

8. Present the pasta on the grand stage, adorned with the remaining truffle slices and a shower of freshly grated Parmigiano Reggiano. Bravo! Enjoy the delicious performance!

Battle of Cheesecakes

Ah, the epic battle of the bakers, Bruno and Bety! It's a culinary clash where sugar and flour meet their match. They've turned our home into a dessert battleground, roping in unsuspecting friends and family as their taste-tester army. Bety, the health guru, dabbles in the art of guilt-free indulgence, while Bruno, our resident mad scientist, creates cake masterpieces that might as well be on a NASA rocket's menu.

But here's the plot twist: now, dear foodie friends, it's your turn to don the judge's hat! Join the sugar-fueled spectacle on Instagram and pick your poison — uh, I mean, recipe. Will it be Bety's virtuous creation or Bruno's intricate dessert extravaganza? The fate of your taste buds rests in your hands!

Bruno's Love-Infused New York'ish Cheesecake Comedy Show

Time:

Prep Time: 20 minutes (or until you've told a cheesy joke)

Bake Time: 10 minutes + 45 minutes + 2 hours (or until your cheesecake is the star of the oven)

Rest/Cool Time: Rest in the fridge during

the evening (because even cheesecakes need beauty sleep)

Ingredients:

For the Base:

- 100g unsalted butter (because every great cheesecake begins with a buttery entrance)
- 150g digestive cookies (the comedic sidekick)
- 1 tbsp of white granulated sugar (for that sweet foundation)

For the Filling:

- 900g of Cream cheese (i.e. Philadelphia, because this is a cream cheese blockbuster)
- 150g of white granulated sugar (for the sweetness that melts hearts)
- 2 tbsp of all-purpose flour (not self-raising flour, because we're not looking for a rising comedy here)
- 1 tsp of vanilla extract (for that vanilla flavor that's not vanilla)
- Zest of 1 lemon (because lemons are the zesty comedians)
- Zest of 1 orange (because oranges are the citrusy performers)
- 3 full eggs (because three's a crowd, but in cheesecakes, it's a party)
- 2 egg yolks (for that extra creamy indulgence)
- 300ml of double cream (because this cheesecake demands double the creaminess)

Note:

> *For the Base:*
> - 100g unsalted butter: Approximately 7 tablespoons

- 150g digestive cookies: Approximately 1.5 cups (crumbs)

For the Filling:
- 900g cream cheese: Approximately 4 cups
- 150g white granulated sugar: Approximately 3/4 cup
- 2 tbsp all-purpose flour: 2 tablespoons
- 1 tsp vanilla extract: 1 teaspoon
- Zest of 1 lemon: Approximately 1 tablespoon
- Zest of 1 orange: Approximately 1 tablespoon
- 3 full eggs: Approximately 1.5 cups (beaten)
- 2 egg yolks: 2 tablespoons
- 300ml double cream: Approximately 1.27 cups

Prep:
1. Heat up the oven to 180°C (because this is where the cheesecake drama begins).
2. Crush the digestive cookies into an almost powder-like consistency. No need to be

homogenous—let there be some comedy in the crumble. Melt the butter in a saucepan on low heat, then mix it with the crushed cookies until well combined.

3. Using a 23cm spring cake tin, spread the mixture to an even layer with the back of a spoon. Put it in the preheated oven at 180°C for 10 minutes. After that, remove it from the oven and let it rest on a cooling rack (because even cheesecake bases need a cool-down).

4. Increase the temperature of the oven to 230°C (the hotter the oven, the cooler the cheesecake).

5. On a kitchen robot (because even robots need a role in the kitchen), beat the cream cheese until smooth (shouldn't take more than 1 or 2 minutes). Slowly add the white sugar and flour, mixing until incorporated and smooth.

6. Increase the speed of the robot and add the vanilla extract, the lemon and orange zest, then add the eggs and egg yolks, one at a time, allowing each one to come together with the mix. Lastly, slowly add the double cream, increasing the speed of the robot if needed. The mix should be light and fluffy (if it's not, you may have added the double cream too fast. The end result will still be good but there is a higher

risk that some of the mix will flow down from the cake tin).

7. By this time, the cookie base should have cooled down. Before adding the mixture, grease the cake tin with butter all around. Make sure you cover all spots to ensure the cheesecake rises well.

8. Add the mixture to the cake tin and use a spatula to make the top even. Put it in the oven for 15 minutes at 230°C. After the 15 minutes pass, lower the temperature to 110°C and cook for an additional 30 minutes. Once the time is over, turn off the oven and let the cheesecake rest there for 2 hours to allow it to cool down and solidify.

9. Remove the cheesecake from the oven, cover it with clean film, and put it in the fridge overnight (because good things come to those who wait).

10. Pass a knife through the sides before opening the spring. In order to come out perfect you can also slightly heat the sides of the cake tin. It's the grand unveiling!

11. Enjoy the show!

Note: For an extra touch of love, you can sprinkle some laughter on top before serving.

Bety's Love-Infused German Cheesecake Spectacle

Preparation: 25 minutes (or until you've practiced your best German cheesecake dance)

Baking Time: 1 hour (or until your cheesecake is as golden as the sun over the Rhine)

Chilling Time: 30 minutes (because even cheesecakes need a chill session)

Quantity: 1 springform (26 cm)

Ingredients:

For the Shortcrust Pastry:

- 200 grams of all-purpose flour (because every great cheesecake starts with a floury entrance)
- 130 grams of cornstarch (because cornstarch is the understated hero)
- 1/2 teaspoon of baking powder (for a cheesecake that rises like a German bread)

- A pinch of salt (just a dash, we're not hosting a salty pretzel show)
- 100 grams of sugar (for that sweet symphony)
- 1 medium-sized egg (because eggs are the comedians of baking)
- 1 medium-sized egg yolk (because yolks need their time in the spotlight)
- 150 grams of cold butter, cut into small pieces (because butter makes everything better)

For the Quark Filling:
- 750 grams of quark, preferably 20% fat; drained (because quark is the rockstar of German cheesecakes)
- 4 medium-sized eggs (for the egg-cellent performance)
- 2 teaspoons of grated lemon zest (for that zesty twist)
- 200 grams of sugar (because sweetness is not optional)
- 2 packets of vanilla pudding powder for cooking (because pudding makes everything smoother)
- 100 milliliters of sunflower oil or rapeseed oil (because even oils have a role to play)

- 300 milliliters of milk (because milk is the backstage crew)

Note:

For the Shortcrust Pastry:
- 200 grams of all-purpose flour: Approximately 1.6 cups
- 130 grams of cornstarch: Approximately 1 cup
- 1/2 teaspoon of baking powder: 1/2 teaspoon
- A pinch of salt: Just a dash (no specific measurement)
- 100 grams of sugar: Approximately 1/2 cup
- 1 medium-sized egg: Approximately 1/4 cup
- 1 medium-sized egg yolk: Approximately 1 tablespoon
- 150 grams of cold butter, cut into small pieces: Approximately 2/3 cup

For the Quark Filling:
- 750 grams of quark: Approximately 3.2 cups

- 4 medium-sized eggs: Approximately 1 cup (beaten)
- 2 teaspoons of grated lemon zest: Approximately 2 lemons' worth
- 200 grams of sugar: Approximately 1 cup
- 2 packets of vanilla pudding powder for cooking: 2 packets
- 100 milliliters of sunflower oil or rapeseed oil: Approximately 1/2 cup
- 300 milliliters of milk: Approximately 1.27 cups

Instructions:

1. Begin by preparing the quark, draining it to reduce moisture. Think of it as quark meditation, finding its center.
2. Line a sieve with a kitchen towel or paper towel, place the quark in it, and position it over the sink or a bowl. This is the quark's spa day.
3. Proceed to make the shortcrust pastry. It's like choreographing a dance = combine flour, cornstarch, baking powder, salt, and sugar in a bowl. Add the eggs and cold butter in small pieces. Use beaters and then your hands to

knead the ingredients into a homogeneous dough. Shape it into a ball, wrap it in plastic wrap, and refrigerate for about 30 minutes. Let the pastry chill, just like a backstage break.

4. Grease the springform and dust it with flour. Preheat the oven to 170 degrees Celsius (Ober- and Unterhitze). Roll out the shortcrust pastry with a rolling pin. It's time to give the pastry a red carpet moment.

5. Line the bottom of the springform with the pastry, creating a raised edge. Think of it as setting the stage for the cheesecake drama. Prick the pastry base with a fork = a little drama before the main act.

6. For the cheesecake filling, whisk the eggs with sugar until fluffy. Stir in the drained quark. Mix in lemon zest, vanilla pudding powder, oil, and milk until no lumps remain. It's the quark's big solo.

7. Pour the cheesecake filling onto the shortcrust pastry in the form. Bake the cake for about 60 to 65 minutes, covering if necessary towards the end. It's the cheesecake's time in the spotlight. Allow it to cool well before cutting = even cheesecakes need a cool-down before their grand entrance.

Notes:

- To prevent the cheese filling from collapsing after baking, perform the following cheesecake magic: After 25 minutes of baking, remove the cake from the oven and loosen the shortcrust edge from the springform edge using a sharp, large knife. Also, lightly score between the still-soft cheesecake filling and the pastry edge with the knife. It's the cheesecake's escape plan. Place the cake back in the oven and bake for another 25 minutes. Repeat the scoring and possibly cover with parchment paper to prevent it from getting too dark. Bake for an additional 15 minutes. It's like directing a cheesecake blockbuster.

- Once the cake is done, let it stand in the turned-off oven for about 30 minutes, with the oven door slightly ajar, using a utensil like a wooden spoon to keep it open. It's the cheesecake's encore moment, basking in the oven's applause.

Enjoy Bety's Love-Infused German Cheesecake Spectacle - a dessert that's a true work of art with a touch of German flair and a whole lot of love!

Pick your favorite kitchen star! Was it the cheesecake that moonwalked into your heart or the quark-filled pastry that did the cha-cha on your taste buds? Spill the beans on Instagram #betyandbruno @betybrunotestkitchen or send a pigeon with your thoughts to betyandbruno@gmail.com. We promise not to judge your favorite based on its dance moves!

Bety's Introduction to Sourdough Bread:

Ah, my days of mischief in Berlin! Amidst the chaos of the pandemic, with supermarket access as rare as a sunny day in November, Bruno and I embarked on a culinary escapade. We dove deep into the art of butter-making, crafted Greek yogurts fit for the gods, and even uncovered the mysteries of Sourdough, thanks to my buddy Jörg's wisdom. That's when my tryst with these tiny bacteria buddies began. The recipes I now share aren't just recipes; they're my Lieblingsrezepte, my favorite secret concoctions from the heart of Berlin's lockdown adventures!

Ah, the sourdough saga! Once I delved into the mysterious world of nurturing that doughy little critter at home, it was like I stumbled into parenthood for carb enthusiasts. Yep, you've got it = sourdough starter is basically a high-maintenance pet with a voracious appetite!

But oh, the reward! That freshly baked sourdough, with its irresistible aroma, is like the siren's call for bread lovers. It lures you in with its heavenly scent, promises satisfaction, and miraculously banishes the incessant cravings for more bread. It's the Gandalf of baked goods, saying, "You shall not pass... another slice!"

Benefits of Sourdough

Sourdough bread is a popular type of bread made through the fermentation of dough using naturally occurring lactobacilli and yeast. This fermentation process offers several benefits that set sourdough apart from other types of bread:

1. **Easier Digestibility:** The fermentation process breaks down gluten and phytic acid, making sourdough easier to digest for people with mild gluten sensitivities. Some individuals who cannot tolerate regular bread find sourdough more manageable.

2. **Lower Glycemic Index:** Sourdough has a lower glycemic index compared to regular bread, which means it has a slower impact on blood sugar levels. This can be particularly beneficial for people with diabetes or those trying to manage their blood sugar levels.

3. **Improved Nutrient Absorption:** The fermentation process in sourdough increases the availability of certain nutrients like vitamins and minerals, making these nutrients easier for

the body to absorb. This can contribute to overall better nutrition.

4. **Reduced Phytic Acid:** Phytic acid, found in many grains, can bind minerals and reduce their absorption in the body. Sourdough's fermentation process reduces the phytic acid content, allowing for better absorption of minerals like calcium, magnesium, and iron.

5. **Richer in Beneficial Compounds:** Sourdough contains various bioactive compounds, including antioxidants and prebiotics, which can have positive effects on overall health. Antioxidants help combat free radicals in the body, potentially reducing the risk of chronic diseases.

6. **Longer Shelf Life:** Sourdough bread tends to have a longer shelf life than bread made with commercial yeast due to its acidic environment, which inhibits the growth of mold and certain bacteria.

7. **Distinct Flavor and Aroma:** Sourdough has a unique tangy flavor and aroma, which many people find appealing. This distinctive taste is a result of the lactic acid produced during the fermentation process.

8. **Artisanal and Natural:** Sourdough is often made using simple ingredients: flour, water, salt, and naturally occurring wild yeast and bacteria. This simplicity and natural fermentation process appeal to individuals seeking a more traditional and artisanal approach to baking.

9. **Potential Gluten Reduction:** While not entirely gluten-free, the fermentation process in sourdough can break down some of the gluten proteins, making it easier to digest for some individuals with mild gluten sensitivities.

It's important to note that while sourdough offers these potential benefits, individual responses to sourdough can vary. People with severe gluten intolerance or celiac disease should still avoid sourdough made from regular wheat flour unless it's specifically labeled and certified as gluten-free.

Bety's Passionately Spelt Sourdough Ballet Buns

Time Prep: 35 minutes (or until your inner baker is warmed up)

Baking Time: 15-18 minutes (because perfection takes its time)

Pre-Dough:

- 165g Spelt flour Type 630 (the prima ballerina of flours)
- 235g Water (because hydration is key)

Bring the water to a boil and pour it over the "measured flour" like a curtain call. Give them a quick knead – think of it as a doughy pas de deux. Store this pre-dough in the refrigerator, covered like a superstar.

Note: I tripled the pre-dough for an encore performance. It can groove in the fridge for up to a week!

Main Dough:

- 960g Spelt flour Type 630 (because we're sticking to the star of the show)
- 560g Water (hydration encore)
- Pre-dough (the opening act)
- 20g Salt (just a pinch, we're not in a salty drama)
- 10g fresh Yeast (because freshness is our leading lady)
- 20g Sourdough starter (the show's starter)
- 40g Liquid malt extract (Alternatively, honey can be used - for that sweet twist)

Note:

For the Pre-Dough:

- 165g Spelt flour Type 630: Approximately 1.3 cups
- 235g Water: 1 cup

For the Main Dough:

- 960g Spelt flour Type 630: Approximately 7.7 cups
- 560g Water: 2.4 cups
- 20g Salt: 1 tablespoon

- 10g fresh Yeast: Approximately 1 tablespoon
- 20g Sourdough starter: Approximately 1.5 tablespoons
- 40g Liquid malt extract: Approximately 2 tablespoons

Bety's Passionately Spelt Sourdough Symphony

Time Prep: 25 minutes (or until your inner dough maestro is warmed up) *Baking Time:* 40-45 minutes (because perfection takes a little longer)

Emmer Rye Sourdough:

- 11g Rye sourdough starter (the tiny maestro of the bread orchestra)
- 110g Water, 40°C (because warm water keeps the sourdough composers cozy)
- 110g Emmer whole grain flour (for the whole-hearted flavor)

Cracked Grain Paste:

- 45g Fine spelt cracked grain (for the crunch that steals the show)
- 0.9g Salt (just a sprinkle, we're not in a salty drama)
- 90g Cold water (because chilled water keeps it cool)

Main Dough:

- Mature Emmer Rye sourdough (the seasoned conductor)
- 120g Cracked grain paste (the crunchy chorus)
- 160g Spelt flour 630 (the prima donna of flours)
- 60g Water (hydration encore)
- 6g Salt (for the salty comedy twist)
- 3g Fresh yeast (because freshness is our leading lady)

Note:

Emmer Rye Sourdough:

- 11g Rye sourdough starter: Approximately 2.75 teaspoons
- 110g Water, 40°C: Approximately 1/2 cup
- 110g Emmer whole grain flour: Approximately 3/4 cup

Cracked Grain Paste:

- 45g Fine spelt cracked grain: Approximately 1/4 cup
- 0.9g Salt: Just a pinch

- 90g Cold water: Approximately 1/3 cup

Main Dough:

- 120g Cracked grain paste: Approximately 1/2 cup
- 160g Spelt flour 630: Approximately 1 1/3 cups
- 60g Water: Approximately 1/4 cup
- 6g Salt: Approximately 1 teaspoon
- 3g Fresh yeast: Approximately 1 teaspoon

These are rough estimates, and the actual cup measurements may vary slightly based on factors like the specific type of ingredient and how it's measured.

Additionally: Spelt flour 630 for dusting (because the stage needs its spotlight)

Instructions:

1. **Emmer Rye Sourdough:** Mix the measured ingredients with a spoon. Cover and let it mature at room temperature (21-22°C) for 12-15 hours. Bread Baking Tip: "If you let the sourdough mature at a warmer temperature (27/28°C), you'll get a sweeter bread. In this case, shorten the resting time a bit."

2. **Cracked Grain Paste:** Put the ingredients in a saucepan, cover, and bring to a boil. Let it simmer gently, stirring occasionally, until a thick porridge forms. Let it cool.

3. **Main Dough (Emmer Rye Mixed Bread):** Put all the ingredients into the machine's bowl. Knead the dough for 8 minutes in the first mixing phase and 5 minutes in the kneading phase until you get a cohesive, slightly sticky dough that doesn't completely detach from the bowl. The dough temperature should be 25-26°C.

4. **Resting Period:** After kneading, cover the dough and let it rest at room temperature for 80 minutes. Interrupt the resting period after 30 and 60 minutes to stretch and fold the dough.

5. **Shaping:** After 80 minutes, place the dough on a floured work surface and gently shape it into a round loaf. Cover with the seam side down and let it rest for 5-10 minutes.

6. **Final Shaping:** Shape the slightly relaxed, rounded dough into a batard and place it in a floured proofing basket for the final proof.

7. **Final Proof:** Let it rise until it's about 3/4 proofed (approximately 1 hour at 33°C, longer at room temperature).

8. **Scoring:** Carefully transfer the proofed dough onto a peel dusted with semolina or flour, seam side down. Make a decorative cut with a sharp knife lengthwise along the loaf.

9. **Baking:** Preheat the oven with a baking stone to 250°C. Bake with steam at 250°C for 8 minutes. After 8 minutes, reduce the temperature to 210°C and bake for 14 minutes. Then, briefly open the oven door to release steam and continue baking at 250°C for 3-5 minutes with the door slightly ajar.

Baking Time: Approximately 25 minutes (because this bread deserves its own spotlight)

Let the 'Emmer Rye Mixed Bread' cool on a wire rack after baking, and enjoy the symphony of flavors!

Bety's Rye Sourdough Bread – "Landbrot": Nostalgia Edition

Time Prep: 25 minutes (or the length of a favorite childhood cartoon) Baking Time: 40-45 minutes (or the duration of a neighborhood hide-and-seek game)

Rye Sourdough:

- 30g Rye sourdough starter (like the secret ingredient in grandma's stories)
- 280g Rye flour 1150 (or alternatively, 997) (because variety is the spice of life)
- 280g Lukewarm water (warmer than a childhood blanket)

Flour Paste:

- 20g Rye flour 1150 (or alternatively, 997) (the magical dust for extra charm)
- 100g Cold water (colder than the ice cream truck's offerings)

Note:

Pre-Dough:

- 165g Spelt flour Type 630 ≈ 1 1/3 cups
- 235g Water ≈ 1 cup

Main Dough:

- 960g Spelt flour Type 630 ≈ 7 2/3 cups
- 560g Water ≈ 2 1/4 cups
- 20g Salt ≈ 4 teaspoons
- 10g fresh Yeast ≈ 3 teaspoons
- 20g Sourdough starter ≈ 1 tablespoon
- 40g Liquid malt extract (Alternatively, honey can be used) ≈ 2 tablespoons

Note: These are rough estimates, and the actual conversion may vary based on the specific ingredient and how you measure it. It's always a good idea to use a kitchen scale for precision.

Main Dough:

- 580g Mature rye sourdough (aged to perfection, like a classic movie)
- 95g Flour paste (the script to our bread drama)
- 130g Rye flour 1150 (or alternatively, 997) (the leading role)

- 180g Wheat flour 550 (or alternatively, 1050 or French T65) (the supporting cast)
- 15g Salt (just enough to spice up the plot)
- 110g Water (the twist in the tale)

Instructions:

1. For the rye sourdough, let the starter tell its tale for 12-15 hours at room temperature. It loves a good bedtime story.
2. For the flour paste, cook up a magical potion of flour and water. Let it cool and keep it in the fridge overnight, like a fairytale elixir.
3. For the main dough, gather all your ingredients for a blockbuster performance. Knead like you're preparing for the grand finale.
4. After the dough rests, shape it into a smooth ball = the hero of our bread saga.
5. Let it rise in the pan, reaching heights like a superhero's leap. Decorate with small incisions = the bread's way of getting into character.
6. Bake with the enthusiasm of a childhood adventure. Steam for a surprise twist, then reduce the heat for the suspenseful climax.

7. Glaze with water = the bread's way of a happy ending.
8. Let it cool for 12 hours on a wire rack, giving it the overnight sleep it deserves = just like a good bedtime story.

Enjoy the nostalgia and let the flavors transport you back to the days of carefree play and simple joys.

First, knead all the ingredients for 6 minutes at a slow speed. Watch out! The dough might seem a bit stiff at first, but it's just warming up. Then, crank up the speed for 2-3 minutes. Keep an eye on it = if the surface starts to shine, it's in danger of being over-kneaded! We don't want a diva dough.

After mixing, let the dough rest for 30 minutes. It's the dough's intermission. After this break, fold the dough once and let it rest for another 20 minutes. A well-rested dough is a happy dough.

Now, divide the dough into 13 equal pieces and shape them into round balls. Let them relax = they've earned it.

Next, shape the dough pieces into hand-shaped Kaiser rolls (see instructions elsewhere = it's like choreographing a bun ballet).

To achieve a beautiful crust, I placed the hand-shaped Kaiser rolls on a tray with the star side facing up. Insufficient crust can often result from handling the dough too much before it goes into the oven! Therefore, I avoid unnecessary handling from the start! We want our buns to shine, not be handled like dough drama queens.

For a strong oven spring, the spelt rolls should be baked at 2/3 proofing. To create a slightly rustic surface, I did NOT spray the pastries with water before baking! Let them rise like true bread stars.

Enjoy the grand performance of Bety's Passionately Spelt Sourdough Ballet Buns – where every bite is a standing ovation!

Bety's Sourdough Bagels: A Dough-lightful Journey to the USA

Prep Time: 25 minutes (because great bagels can't be rushed, just like a scenic road trip)

Cook Time: 35 minutes (for that perfect bake, like hitting all the must-see landmarks)

Fermentation Time: 12 hours (letting the flavors ferment like memories from a cross-country adventure)

Total Time: 13 hours (because every good journey needs time to savor)

Servings: 16 (enough to share with newfound friends)

Ingredients:

For the Sourdough Starter:

- 30 g (30 g) sourdough starter (the captain of this flavorful expedition)

- 100 g (100 g) all-purpose flour (the co-pilot of our dough plane)
- 100 g (100 g) water (the refreshing pitstop)

For the Bagel Dough:
- 200 g (200 g) active sourdough starter (because a lively starter is the heartbeat of great bagels)
- 510 g (510 g) water (keeping the dough hydrated for the journey)
- 80 g (80 g) honey or sugar (for a sweet touch, just like Southern hospitality)
- 20 g (20 g) fine sea salt (because every adventure needs a bit of saltiness)
- 1000 g (1000 g) bread flour (the sturdy vehicle for our bagel journey)

For the Water Bath:
- 12 cups water (for a refreshing soak, like dipping our toes in the Atlantic)
- 2 tablespoons granulated sugar (a sweet addition, just like a sweet roadside find)

Note:

Sourdough Starter:

- 30 g sourdough starter ≈ 2 tablespoons
- 100 g all-purpose flour ≈ 3/4 cup
- 100 g water ≈ 1/2 cup

Bagel Dough:

- 200 g active sourdough starter ≈ 1 cup
- 510 g water ≈ 2 1/4 cups
- 80 g honey or sugar ≈ 1/4 cup
- 20 g fine sea salt ≈ 1 tablespoon
- 1000 g bread flour ≈ 7 1/2 cups

Water Bath:

- 12 cups water ≈ 3 cups
- 2 tablespoons granulated sugar ≈ 1/4 cup

Optional Toppings:

- sesame seeds (the travelers' choice, like a road trip playlist)
- Everything Bagel Seasoning (for those who want a bit of everything, just like exploring every corner)

- salt sprinkle on top, don't dip (for the minimalist adventurer)
- poppy seeds (a classic choice, like the iconic Route 66)
- shredded cheese (because cheese makes everything better, just like a cheesy roadside attraction)

Instructions:

Feed Your Sourdough Starter: 12 hours before our bagel journey, wake up the starter and let it rise, just like the sun over the Grand Canyon.

Make the Dough: Mix, knead, and let it rest—like a good night's sleep before hitting the road.

Shape and Rise: Divide, shape, and let them rise, just like the excitement building up before a road trip.

Boil and Toppings: Boil the bagels, the way we dive into adventures. Add toppings for a personal touch, like customizing your travel itinerary.

Bake: In the oven, let them bake to golden perfection, like reaching your destination after a satisfying journey.

Enjoy your Bety's Sourdough Bagels - a taste of the USA in every bite! Share your bagel tales with #BetyBagelAdventure! 🚗☐

Bruno's Spaghetti Carbonara - the dish that is the best original

Time Prep: In the time it takes for you to practice your stand-up routine, approximately 30 minutes.

Ingredients:

- 250g Spaghettoni (because ordinary spaghetti is so last season)
- 150g Guanciale (the bacon's cooler Italian cousin)
- 75g Pecorino Romano (for that sheepish charm)
- 50g Parmigiano Reggiano (because two cheeses are better than one)
- 3 Egg Yolks (because eggs are the performers of this culinary stage)
- Water from the pasta cooking (where the magic happens)
- Black Pepper to taste (the spice that adds the punchline)

Note:

- 250g Spaghettoni: Approximately 2 cups
- 150g Guanciale: Approximately 1 cup
- 75g Pecorino Romano: Approximately 1 cup (grated)
- 50g Parmigiano Reggiano: Approximately 1/2 cup (grated)
- 3 Egg Yolks: Approximately 1/2 cup
- Water from the pasta cooking: This is a liquid measure, and 100ml to 150ml is approximately 1/2 to 2/3 cup.
- Black Pepper to taste: As per personal preference, but roughly 2 tablespoons, if coarsely ground.

These are rough estimates as the conversion from grams to cups can vary based on factors like the ingredient's density and how it's packed. Cooking is both science and art, after all! Adjustments may be needed based on your taste preferences. Enjoy your Spaghettoni Carbonara!

Preparation:

1. Start with the guanciale - it's like peeling off the tough exterior to reveal the true character. Remove the thick skin and cut it into one-centimeter chunks. Throw it into a hot pan; no need for oil – guanciale is the diva that releases its own drama (and fat). Cook until it becomes the rockstar of crispiness. Strain the released fat, but don't bid it farewell; it's got an encore coming up.

2. Boil water in a pan, add Spaghettoni, and let it cook until "al dente." You want a pasta that still has a bit of a punchline when you bite into it.

3. While Spaghettoni struts its stuff, whisk together egg yolks, Pecorino Romano, Parmigiano Reggiano, and black pepper. Add half of the reserved guanciale fat. Timing is crucial, like a perfectly timed punchline. Around 6 minutes into Spaghettoni's performance, add some pasta water to the egg mixture – whisk vigorously to avoid an egg comedy routine. You're aiming for a thin liquid, not an omelette (think 100-150ml water).

4. Strain the pasta, but save some water – it's not just a prop, you might need it. Add the pasta to

the guanciale pan, turn the heat to low, pour in the egg mixture, and blend it all together. Turn off the heat, add most of the fried guanciale – you're going for creamy pasta with sauce that steals the show. If it's too dry, cue the pasta water to the rescue.

5. Serve with a sprinkle of Pecorino Romano on top. It's not just dinner; it's a culinary comedy extravaganza. Enjoy the delicious punchlines!

Bruno's Duck Magret

Welcome to Duck Magret Mastery – where simplicity meets succulence! This dish is so easy, even the ducks are quacking about it.

Time Prep: 25m

Ingredients:

- 2 Duck breasts with skin
- Salt & Black Pepper

Preparation:

1. Crank up the oven to a toasty 200°Celsius. It's about to get quackers!

2. Wipe down those duck breasts like you're cleaning a rare jewel. Season them with a sprinkle of salt and a generous grind of black pepper. The ducks approve.

3. Grab a pan that's oven-bound or pop an oven tray inside to get it heated. Now, place the duck breasts skin-side down on the cold pan. Cold is

the new hot = it lets the fat do a little dance before crisping up.

4. Crank up the heat, and watch the fat groove out of the duck. Let it sizzle on the skin side until it's crispy and brown, around 4 to 5 minutes. Keep an eye on it; you're not filming a cooking marathon.

5. Flip the duck, give the other side a little tan for 1 to 2 minutes until it's golden brown.

6. Exit stage left from the heat, turn the fat side down, and waltz it into the preheated oven for 7 minutes.

7. Curtain call! Take it out, let it rest on a cutting board for 7m. Precision is key; we're crafting duck art here.

8. Slice it up into approximately 1 centimeter pieces. Duck, duck, voilà!

9. Serve it with mashed potatoes because, as the saying goes, ducks of a feather flock together.

Bruno's Salmon with Sweet Potato

Now, for Bruno's Salmon with Sweet Potato, we're diving into a sea of flavor!

Time Prep: 60m

Ingredients:

- 2 large sweet potatoes (orange, because they know how to stand out)
- 1 Red onion (for the onion-tainment)
- 1 Garlic bulb (because vampires are not invited)
- Thyme, Salt, Black Pepper, olive oil (the symphony of flavors)
- 1 Salmon tail, open in half, bones removed (salmonella not included)

Preparation:

1. Heat things up to a fiery 200°Celsius in the oven. It's getting hot in here!

2. Peel those sweet potatoes and chop them into squares – we're talking 1-centimeter squares, not geometry class. Toss them on an oven tray, coat them in olive oil, and season like it's a food carnival – salt, black pepper, and a sprinkle of thyme confetti.

3. Cut that onion (cue the tears of joy), break up the garlic bulb (vampires, beware), and throw them into the sweet potato fiesta.

Cod Adventure in the Land of Saudade: Bacalhau à Brás

Time Prep: 30m

Ingredients:

- Fresh parsley (because every dish needs a sprig of freshness)

- Potatoes (800g, or as we like to call them, the starchy comedians)
- Soaked cod fillet (500g, the star of our saudade show)
- Olive oil (2 tbsp., the smooth operator)
- Garlic (4 cloves, bringing the aromatic drama)
- Bay leaf (1 leaf, a prop for our saudade play)
- Eggs (6, the versatile performers)
- Onion (1 unit, our supporting character)

Preparation:

1. *Cod Chronicles:* Cook the cod and let it cool = give it a moment to ponder its aquatic adventures.

2. *Potato Pizzazz:* Peel the potatoes and cut them into very thin sticks, creating a stage for our saudade straw potatoes. Soak them to remove excess gum — no sticky situations here!

3. *Cod Unveiling:* Remove the cod's skin and bones, shred it with the flair of a dramatic saudade gesture.

4. *Potato Drama Continues:* Drain and dry the potatoes. Fry them in heated oil, turning them into golden strands of saudade.

5. *Onion Opera:* Heat oil in a pan, sauté sliced onion, garlic, and the bay leaf = a symphony of sizzling saudade.

6. *Cod Reunion:* Add shredded cod, let the saudade unfold, cooking until it turns white.

7. *Potato Encore:* Remove the bay leaf, introduce the fries, a saudade spectacle in the making.

8. *Egg Extravaganza:* Beat the eggs, gently stir, let them coat the saudade ensemble. Don't let them cook too much; we want a saudade silkiness.

9. *Finale Flourish:* Sprinkle with parsley, our
    saudade confetti, and decorate with olives — a
    grand saudade performance awaits!

And there you have it — Bacalhau a la Saudade! A
culinary comedy served with a side of Portuguese
nostalgia. Obrigado for the saudade feast! 🎭🐟

Bruno's and Bety's Neapolitan Pizza Dough: A Tale of Love and Drama

Time Prep: 24h (includes rest time) Baking time: +- 10m at 250°C

Ingredients:

For the Poolish (Cue the Opera Music):

- 300gr type 00" flour (the leading flour in our culinary drama)
- 300ml water at room temperature (aqua amore)
- 5gr of fresh yeast (the yeast that rises above all)
- 3gr of honey (a touch of sweetness in our tragic tale)

For the Dough (Enter the Protagonist):

- 400gr type 00" flour (the star of our pizza opera)
- 190ml water at room temperature (a supporting role for hydration)
- 20gr of fine salt (the dramatic seasoning)
- 15gr of virgin olive oil (the smooth operator)

Note:

For the Poolish

- 300 grams of type 00" flour ≈ 2.4 cups
- 300 milliliters of water at room temperature ≈ 1.27 cups
- 5 grams of fresh yeast ≈ 1.25 teaspoons
- 3 grams of honey ≈ 0.9 teaspoons

For the Dough

- 400 grams of type 00" flour ≈ 3.2 cups
- 190 milliliters of water at room temperature ≈ 0.8 cups
- 20 grams of fine salt ≈ 3.2 teaspoons
- 15 grams of virgin olive oil ≈ 1.3 tablespoons

Preparation:

Act 1 - The Poolish Drama (Start 24h Before):

1. Dissolve 5gr of fresh yeast in 300ml of water, add 3gr of honey = a prelude to passion.
2. Mix flour, creating a symphony of flavors. Let it rest for 1 hour, a calm before the storm.
3. Move the mixture to the fridge for a chilling twist, 16-24 hours of anticipation.

Act 2 - The Dough Dilemma (3 Hours Before Pizza Curtain):

1. Take the poolish from the fridge = a cold-hearted twist.
2. Mix it with water, a hand-whisked ballet of emotions.
3. Slowly add flour = a delicate dance of incorporation.
4. Increase the mixer speed, add salt, cue the intensity.
5. Add olive oil, let it beat = a crescendo of passion for 10m.
6. Flour the counter = a sprinkle of hope.
7. Cut into 280gr = characters take shape.
8. Let it double = a rising action of anticipation.

Act 3 - The Pizza Performance:

1. Stretch the dough, a metaphorical journey from the center to the edges.
2. Be creative with toppings - but, ah, the tragic pineapple, is forbidden in this Italian drama!

Finale - Curtain Call: As the pizza emerges from the fiery oven, let the curtain fall. A round of applause for Bruno's and Bety's Neapolitan Pizza Dough, a culinary masterpiece filled with love, drama, and the forbidden fruit of pizza ingredients. Bravo!

Benefits of Poolish

Poolish is a pre-ferment used in bread baking, typically made with equal parts flour and water and a small amount of yeast. Allowing this mixture to ferment for a specific period results in a bubbly, flavorful starter that enhances the quality of bread in various ways. Here are some benefits of using poolish in bread baking:

1. **Improved Flavor:** Poolish contributes a mild, slightly tangy flavor to bread. The fermentation process enhances the taste by breaking down

complex compounds in the flour, resulting in a richer and more nuanced flavor profile in the final bread.

2. **Better Texture:** Poolish helps improve the texture of bread by enhancing its crumb structure. The fermentation process creates air pockets in the dough, leading to a lighter, airier, and more tender interior.

3. **Extended Shelf Life:** Due to the pre-fermentation process, poolish bread tends to have a longer shelf life. The fermentation breaks down starches into simpler sugars, providing a natural preservative effect that helps keep the bread fresh for a longer time.

4. **Natural Leavening:** Poolish acts as a natural leavening agent. While commercial yeast can also provide leavening, poolish gives the bread a more complex and interesting flavor compared to using only commercial yeast.

5. **Enhanced Aroma:** The fermentation of poolish produces aromatic compounds that contribute to a pleasant, appetizing smell in the bread. This aroma is often described as slightly nutty and slightly sweet.

6. **Digestibility:** Just like other pre-ferments, poolish contributes to the breakdown of gluten

and phytic acid during fermentation. This can make the bread more digestible for individuals with mild gluten sensitivities and can also improve the absorption of nutrients.

7. **Versatility:** Poolish can be used in various types of bread, including baguettes, rustic loaves, ciabatta, and more. Its versatility allows bakers to experiment with different recipes and create a wide range of bread textures and flavors.

8. **Traditional Baking Technique:** Poolish is a traditional French method that adds an element of authenticity to bread baking. Using poolish can be a way for bakers to connect with time-honored baking traditions.

It's important to note that while poolish offers these benefits, it requires proper management of fermentation time and temperature to achieve the desired results. Additionally, poolish is not gluten-free, so individuals with severe gluten intolerance or celiac disease should avoid bread made with poolish unless specifically labeled and certified as gluten-free.

Final Words

Benefits of baking and cooking with passion and love

Baking and cooking with passion and love can transform the entire culinary experience, not just for the chef but also for those who get to enjoy the food. Here's how infusing passion and love into the cooking process can be incredibly beneficial:

1. **Enhanced Flavor:** When you cook with passion and love, you are more likely to pay attention to the details such as seasoning, choosing fresh ingredients, and experimenting with flavors. This attention to detail often results in dishes that are rich, flavorful, and well-balanced.

2. **Positive Energy:** Cooking with passion and love infuses positive energy into the food. People often say that you can taste the chef's emotions in their dishes. A positive, loving attitude while cooking can make the meal more enjoyable and satisfying for those who eat it.

3. **Creative Expression:** Cooking with passion allows for creative expression. Chefs and home cooks alike can experiment with ingredients, techniques, and presentation, resulting in unique and innovative dishes that reflect their personality and style.

4. **Nourishment for the Soul:** Food prepared with love and passion can be deeply nourishing not just for the body but also for the soul. Sharing a homemade meal that you've put your heart into can create a sense of connection and warmth among family and friends.

5. **Stress Reduction:** Engaging in the cooking process with passion can serve as a form of stress relief. Focusing on the task at hand, enjoying the sensory experiences, and creating something beautiful and delicious can be therapeutic and calming.

6. **Improved Skills:** When you're passionate about cooking, you're more likely to invest time in learning new techniques, recipes, and cuisines. This continuous learning enhances your culinary skills, allowing you to create more diverse and impressive dishes.

7. **Cultural Connection:** Passionate cooking often involves exploring different cuisines and

culinary traditions. This not only broadens your culinary knowledge but also fosters an appreciation for different cultures and their unique food practices.

8. **Encourages Mindfulness:** Being passionate about cooking encourages mindfulness. It prompts you to be present in the moment, focusing on the smells, tastes, and textures. This mindfulness can enhance the overall cooking experience and the enjoyment of the final dish.

9. **Generosity and Sharing:** When you cook with love and passion, you are more likely to share your creations with others. This act of generosity can strengthen relationships and create a sense of community and togetherness.

In summary, cooking and baking with passion and love elevates the entire cooking process, resulting in delicious, soul-nourishing meals that have the power to bring people together and create lasting memories.

Bety and Bruno's Personal Secret Ingredients

Ah, in every recipe, there's a dash of our soul, a sprinkle of our deepest cravings. It's like we're pouring our hearts onto the plate, infusing the dish with all the things we adore. The tangy embrace of sourdough, the earthy allure of truffles, the creamy richness of avocado, the dreamy decadence of sour cream — each ingredient tells a story, evokes a memory, and adds a touch of our essence to the mix. It's not just about taste; it's about the emotions stirred with every whisk, every fold, and every sizzle in the pan. These ingredients are more than flavors; they're fragments of our passions, folded gently into the recipe, transforming a mere dish into a symphony of our deepest culinary desires.

Where to find the ingredients:

In our quest for culinary nirvana, we embarked on a journey of passion, fine-tuning our recipes with the precision of a chemist and the heart of an artist. We scoured the globe for the finest ingredients - flour meticulously milled in the heart of Germany, pizza flour and tomatoes kissed by the Italian sun, and herbs nurtured in our very own garden.

But here's the exciting bit: we're not just hoarding these gastronomic treasures for ourselves! We're considering sharing the wealth. Your feedback is our secret ingredient. Tell us what you think, and who knows? Soon, you might find a slice of Italy or a pinch of German craftsmanship delivered right to your doorstep. It's not just a meal; it's a global taste adventure, and you're invited!

Loved our recipes? Have a question?

Get in contact with us through email:
betyandbruno@gmail.com

or

Instagram @betybrunotestkitchen

Milton Keynes UK
Ingram Content Group UK Ltd.
UKHW022135270624
444694UK00016B/87